BATTLE FOR TIME

BATTLE FOR TIME

AN UNOFFICIAL MINECRAFTERS TIME TRAVEL ADVENTURE

BOOK SIX

Winter Morgan

Sky Pony Press
New York

Sky Pony Press books may be purchased in bulk at special discounts for sales promotion, corporate gifts, fund-raising, or educational purposes. Special editions can also be created to specifications. For details, contact the Special Sales Department, Sky Pony Press, 307 West 36th Street, 11th Floor, New York, NY 10018 or info@skyhorsepublishing.com.

Visit our website at www.skyponypress.com.

10 9 8 7 6 5 4 3 2 1

Library of Congress Cataloging-in-Publication Data is available on file.

Cover design by Brian Peterson
Cover art by Megan Miller

Print ISBN: 978-1-5107-4119-5
E-book ISBN: 978-1-5107-4132-4

Printed in the United States of America

TABLE OF CONTENTS

BATTLE FOR TIME

1
ROOFTOP FARM

"Are you ready? Can I see the farm?" Poppy called out from the stairwell leading to the roof of the new skyscraper she had just built. Poppy had also designed a large glass viewing area on the roof where visitors could see all of Meadow Mews and even parts of Verdant Valley. She was happy to have completed the building and was excited for the grand opening celebrations later that week. People from across the Overworld were coming to the grand opening. When Poppy thought about this, she had butterflies in her stomach. She had never created a structure that was this big, and the idea that so many people would be celebrating a work she created made Poppy excited, but also anxious.

Poppy felt the highlight of the building was the enormous rooftop farm, where folks who worked and stayed in the skyscraper could pick fresh fruit. She hadn't designed it. In fact, she hadn't even seen it. Her friends Brett and Joe told her she couldn't see the rooftop farm until they were finished, and today was the day she would finally see the farm.

Poppy had been waiting in the stairwell for what felt like an eternity, and she wanted to see the farm. Brett and Joe had been working on it nonstop, and she had heard snippets of conversations they'd had about the farm, but she never even got a peek at the plans. Poppy called out again, "Is it ready?"

"You need patience," her friend Nancy said as she walked toward the stairway. Although Nancy was a treasure hunter, she also knew a bit about farming and helped Brett and Joe with the final touches. She adjusted her wool hat as she spoke. "We want everything to be perfect for you. We know how much this means to you."

"I know," Poppy said with a sigh. "It just feels like I've been waiting forever. I can't wait to see the farm."

She heard Brett's voice in the distance, "Almost ready. Just hold on a few more minutes."

Nancy tried to distract Poppy with small talk, but Poppy wasn't interested.

"I hear there will be hundreds of people arriving tomorrow," said Nancy. "I actually saw a few arriving today. They came by boat. At first I thought they were pirates."

"Pirates!" Poppy shrieked.

"No, I thought they were pirates because they were all dressed in blue and they had their swords out, but when I approached them they told me they were here for the grand opening and they put their swords back in their inventories. They explained that their ship had been attacked at sea and they were still nervous." Nancy said this all in one breath and exhaled.

"Should we be worried? Perhaps the people who attacked their ship will dock at Meadow Mews?" Poppy questioned. She was worried that there would be an incident that might destroy the grand opening festivities because several times when they were constructing the building, they had found bricks of TNT. The town had put together a makeshift police force led by their friend Helen. Nancy was also a member of this police force.

"I don't think we should be worried. I spoke with these visitors at great length, and they were attacked in the middle of the sea, far from Meadow Mews. They were so excited to see the building. One of them was a builder, and he wanted to meet with you," said Nancy.

Poppy's heart beat fast. She wasn't a fan of discussing her work. She liked to build, but she wasn't the type to go over every detail about her projects. Poppy preferred for visitors to enjoy what she built rather than questioning its construction.

Brett jogged over and announced, "We're ready!"

Poppy raced past the glass viewing area and toward the farm. She exclaimed, "Oh my! This is beyond incredible." She saw the lush leafy trees filled with ripe apples and the rows of potatoes and wheat. "This can feed our entire village."

"It was designed to feed everyone in this building," remarked Brett. "This is a large building. In fact, there are more rooms in this building than homes in our community."

Poppy never realized how massive the skyscraper was until Brett mentioned this perspective. She began to question if she had made the right decision. Was creating a building that was essentially larger than their small town a bad idea? She hoped this wouldn't change the atmosphere of Meadow Mews. She loved the fact that she knew everyone in town, but she also was happy that Meadow Mews was growing. The skyscraper was a sign that Meadow Mews was advancing. She knew that it had a long history and the founder, Grant, would have been happy to know that this structure was attracting people from around the Overworld. Meadow Mews was now a destination point on the map. Any idea that she had made a bad decision vanished as she walked through the rows of wheat growing atop the building.

"You guys did the best job. I can't believe how well everything is growing," Poppy marveled as she picked an apple from a tree and took a bite.

"We are closer to the sun," Brett said as he pointed at the hot sun that beat down on the roof.

"True," Poppy said and then remarked, "I should have built a covering so people could be in the shade while they ate the fruit and vegetables from the farm."

Poppy was always adding to buildings and structures she had designed. She believed her work was never done and there were always improvements to be made.

"We are so glad you like the farm." Joe smiled. "You did such a great job with this building that we wanted to create a farm that would be worthy of being on this well-designed rooftop."

Poppy blushed. "Please," she said with a nervous chuckle, "the only reason people will even want to come here is for this vibrant farm."

They heard voices in the distance, and Poppy turned around. She spotted four people dressed in blue. Nancy said, "Those are the visitors from the boat. I have no idea how they got up here. Nobody is supposed to be up here until the celebration." Nancy hurried over to the visitors.

One of the people dressed in blue rushed right over to Poppy. "Are you the one who designed this marvelous structure?"

Poppy didn't have time to answer. One of the other people from the group that was dressed in blue called out, "She is."

Before Poppy could even let out a scream, the four strangers surrounded her, and pointing their swords at her unarmored chest, they said, "You're coming with us."

2
VISITORS

Brett, Joe, and Nancy sprinted toward Poppy's captors, but the blue army of invaders sprinkled a potion of invisibility on Poppy and themselves.

"Where are they?" screamed Brett.

"I can't see them!" hollered Joe.

Nancy charged toward the stairs, grabbing at the air, hoping she could get hold of someone, but there was nobody there. The gang was beginning to lose hope when they heard someone scream.

"Leave me alone!" the voice demanded.

Brett pointed. "Look, there's a sword!"

Poppy had struck one of the attackers, but since they were invisible, only the swords were visible. Brett wanted to chuckle as he watched the swords clashing, because seeing swords floating in space was an odd sight. Yet Brett remembered that his best friend was holding one of these swords and was fighting a battle against four people. He had no reason to chuckle. He had to save Poppy.

"Poppy!" Brett screamed.

Poppy and the four invaders were battling beside a row of wheat, and one captor's sword fell atop the wheat. Brett lunged and grabbed the sword.

"Give it back," the voice demanded.

"Poppy," Brett said, "please stand next to me. I want to know which one you are."

Brett could feel somebody grab his arm. "I'm right here."

As Brett began to strike the person he believed was in front of him, the potion wore off. He slammed his sword into one of Poppy's captors, and they were destroyed. Nancy and Joe raced over with their diamond swords and attacked the remaining three people dressed in blue. When there was only one blue villain remaining, Poppy instructed her friends, "Stop! Let him live. I have questions to ask him."

The remaining captor shook. He had one heart left, and he was nervous. "What do you want to know?"

Tears filled Poppy's eyes, and she asked, "Why?"

"It was orders," he replied.

"From who?" asked Brett.

"Our leader."

"Who is that?" asked Brett.

"Where are you from?" asked Poppy.

"We are from the —" but before the captor could answer, he was struck with an arrow and destroyed.

Poppy turned around and shrieked, "Skeletons!"

The sun was setting, and a skeleton army had spawned on the roof of the skyscraper. The gang put on their armor and readied themselves for an attack on the skeletons. Arrows flew through the sky, and the gang leaped toward the bony beasts and destroyed the skeletons.

Rattling bones were heard as they annihilated the final skeletons. When the last skeleton was obliterated, Poppy grabbed an apple from a tree and took a bite. She had a low health bar, and she needed nourishment.

"Guys," she said to her friends, "I am really worried about the grand opening. This was supposed to be a time of celebration, but now I'm too nervous to enjoy it. What if these people come back and want to capture me again?"

"We will protect you," said Brett.

Joe and Nancy agreed they wouldn't leave Poppy's side until they figured out who was behind the attack and were able to stop them.

Nancy looked at the sky. "It's getting very dark. The sun is basically set, and if we don't get to shelter soon, we will be attacked by more hostile mobs."

Poppy suggested they stay at the hotel in the skyscraper. "I'm afraid to go home," she confessed. "I worry that they will be waiting for me."

Brett agreed, and they walked into the hotel and found a room for four people. They climbed into the beds and pulled their wool blankets over them. Poppy didn't feel as if she could sleep. Her mind was racing.

She kept going over what weapons she had in her inventory in case the blue-clad strangers returned in the middle of the night. She kept her eye on the door as she got up from the bed and began to pace in the small hotel room.

"Poppy," Brett whispered, "are you okay?"

"No." She got back into bed. "I'm really scared."

"It will be okay," Brett said. "You get some sleep, and I will keep an eye on the door. If they break in, I will attack them. You need to be rested. Tomorrow is your big day."

"Thank you," Poppy said as she closed her eyes.

When Poppy awoke, she heard Brett talking to Helen. "Helen?" Poppy sat up in bed. "What are you doing here?"

"I came to wake you guys up," Helen explained. "There are lots of visitors checking into the hotel, and we need this room for them. Also there is press here. They want to interview you about the new skyscraper."

"Is the grand opening celebration still happening?" asked Poppy.

"Yes," said Helen. "Why would we cancel it?"

Brett explained that Poppy had been attacked by people on the rooftop, and Helen let out a gasp. "That's awful. I will make sure we have more security."

Poppy took a sip of milk and then asked, "Do I really have to talk to reporters about my skyscraper?"

"Yes," said Helen, "it would be nice. They traveled here to see you."

Brett walked over to Poppy. "I just want you to

know that I will be beside you all day. I am going to make sure nothing happens to you."

"Thank you," she said with a smile.

"Are you ready?" asked Helen.

Poppy, Brett, Nancy, and Joe followed Helen outside of the room. They were shocked to see the halls filled with people. Visitors from across the Overworld had arrived and were ready to celebrate the grand opening of the hotel. The only person who didn't feel like celebrating was Poppy.

As they made their way outside of the hotel, Poppy spotted familiar faces in the crowd.

"Look!" she called out to Brett, Joe, and Nancy. "It's the guys in blue!"

3
IT'S A CELEBRATION

Brett bolted toward the people dressed in blue. "You must leave Meadow Mews now," he demanded.

They appeared confused and didn't respond.

"You have to go," Brett said.

"Why?" asked one of the people in blue.

"Yesterday you tried to capture the person who built this skyscraper," Brett explained, "and we can't have you here at the celebration."

"We never did that," said one of the people dressed in blue.

Brett called for help, and Joe and Nancy hurried over. Nancy demanded the invaders leave the celebration. Crowds formed around them as the people in blue raised their voices and took out their swords.

"What do you want from Poppy?" Brett asked them.

They didn't respond. One of them swung his sword at Brett, and it landed in Brett's shoulder. He cried out in pain as he lost a heart. Nancy leaped at Brett's attacker. As Nancy ripped through his chest, a loud noise was heard.

"What was that?" Joe asked nervously.

They turned around and let out a collective gasp when they saw a gaping hole in the front of the skyscraper's first floor.

The people in blue escaped amid the smoke as the crowds fled from the burning skyscraper.

"We have to find them," Nancy called out.

"No, I want to see if Poppy is okay," said Brett.

Smoke rose from the building. Joe said, "I bet there's TNT all around the skyscraper. We have to go search."

Brett, Joe, and Nancy raced through the smoky air searching for Poppy, but they couldn't see her. As they approached the building, a second explosion shook the ground. Brett looked up and cried out, "Oh no!"

The second floor of the skyscraper was destroyed. Nancy said, "Poppy worked so hard on this building. Who would do something like this?"

Brett spotted Poppy in the distance, and he hurried toward her. "Poppy!"

Poppy was standing with Helen by the podium that was set up in front of the building. Poppy was to deliver a speech at the grand opening ceremony. Instead of addressing the crowd about the building, she stood by the podium staring at the skyscraper in disbelief.

Brett ran to Poppy. She looked at him and asked, "How did this happen?"

"You can fix this," he told her. "I know it. You are the best builder in the Overworld. There is obviously someone out there who wants to destroy your building, but we aren't going to let them. We will stop them, and you will rebuild."

"I hope you're right," said Poppy.

"I know I am. I believe in you, and I believe in this building," said Brett, but as those words fell from his lips, another explosion was heard.

The gang stared at the building, but they didn't see any damage. Nancy asked, "What happened? I don't see anything."

"Over there," Brett said as he noticed a large crater in the ground. A large group of people clustered around the crater and stared at the hole in the ground.

Brett rushed toward the crowd, made his way to the front, and looked down at the hole. It looked like a never-ending tunnel. Joe stood beside him and asked, "Do you feel the cold air emanating from the tunnel?"

Brett could feel goose bumps on his arms. "Yes," he replied.

Joe ordered everyone to stand back. He had felt this cold before, and he knew that this was probably a portal. He didn't want these innocent bystanders to fall into another time period. He also had no idea how he could explain this to them.

"You have to stand back," Joe said. "We don't want you falling into this massive hole in the ground."

Brett added, "Everyone should leave the area. It's very dangerous, and we don't want anyone getting hurt."

A reporter wearing a fedora and a brown blazer spotted Poppy walking toward Brett and ran over to her, overwhelming Poppy with questions.

"Did you have any warning that something like this might happen? Do you have any idea who might be behind these attacks? Are you planning to rebuild?"

Poppy had no answers. She just stared at her work of art and cried. "I don't know why anyone would do this to the skyscraper or why someone would attack the peaceful town of Meadow Mews. I built this skyscraper so people from across the Overworld could enjoy it, not destroy it."

The reporter didn't take notes. He just listened, as he saw the pained expression on Poppy's face. While Poppy explained how devastated she was about the explosion, a thunderous boom was heard, and the crowd jumped.

Everyone was relieved as rain fell upon the crowd. Poppy said, "Thankfully this wasn't another explosion."

Poppy wanted to run back to the skyscraper to search the building for TNT. She didn't want another attack to happen. The damage on the first two floors was an easy repair, but if more TNT exploded, she worried that she wouldn't be able to save the building. Poppy thought about the rooftop farm and all of the amenities the building had, and she started to race toward it. She had to save the building. She had worked hard to create this skyscraper, and she wasn't going to let anyone destroy it.

Her feet were drenched as she ran through puddles. She stopped short when two arrows stung her arm. Poppy looked up to see several skeletons and zombies attacking the crowds.

Brett called out, "Poppy! Where are you going?"

"I have to save the skyscraper," she cried out.

Brett said, "I'll help you," and handed her a potion to regain her strength and instructed her to drink it.

As they raced toward the skyscraper, they could hear Joe cry out, "Help me!" They turned around to see Joe and Nancy in a serious battle with the skeletons. If Joe moved back a step, he would fall into the hole in the ground. The rain was falling harder, and another thunderous boom shook the ground. Brett watched as Joe fell into the portal.

Poppy said, "We have to save Joe!"

Brett and Poppy dodged a barrage of arrows as they made their way toward the hole in the ground. Brett could feel the chill as he approached the hole. He held Poppy's hand as they jumped into the portal together.

4
COLD ARRIVAL

No matter how many times Brett fell through a portal, he would never get used to the cold. This time the cold, coupled with his wet T-shirt, made him feel as if he were turning into an icicle. He couldn't think about himself, though; he was too concerned with finding Joe when he entered whatever time period this portal decided to throw him in. The trip through this portal felt longer than the others. Brett felt as if he had been falling in this cold darkness forever. When he jumped into the portal, he was holding Poppy's hand, but the wind had broken them apart, and she fell below him. Brett feared he'd land on her when he emerged in this new land.

"Poppy," Brett called out, but there was no response.

After a few minutes, Brett heard someone faintly call his name. It didn't sound like Poppy, but it sounded familiar. Another burst of cold rushed through the portal, and Brett's teeth chattered. He was about to lose consciousness due to the frigid conditions when he landed on the ground with a plop.

Brett made an imprint in the snow when he landed. *Oh great*, he said to himself. *There's no way I will warm up here.*

Brett looked around at the miles of snow that stood before him. In the distance he could see a large igloo. He grabbed a bottle of milk to regain his strength and then walked toward the igloo. As he trekked through the snow, he called out for his friends, Joe and Poppy, but they were nowhere in sight, and Brett was worried. He didn't understand why they hadn't landed in the same spot that he did.

A voice called out in the distance, "Excuse me. Friend of Poppy's. Excuse me."

Brett turned around and recognized the reporter in the fedora and brown blazer.

"What's your name?" the reporter asked as he approached Brett.

"Brett. Yours?"

"Pete," the reporter replied.

"Did you follow us in the portal?" asked Brett.

"Yes," Pete said, "but I didn't know it was a portal. I had no idea what I was jumping into when I ran after Poppy."

"Why did you run after Poppy?" asked Brett.

"I had to. I was writing a story about her."

"Wow, you really make sacrifices for your job." Brett couldn't believe Pete was that brave.

"Where's Poppy?" asked Pete.

Brett looked around, but all he saw was ice, snow, and the igloo in the distance. He didn't know where Poppy or Joe were, and he was concerned. It made no sense. How could Pete be in this biome, but Joe and Poppy were missing? He looked at the snow and replied, "I don't know and I'm worried."

"Don't worry. We'll find her," Pete reassured Brett.

Brett pointed at the igloo in the distance. "I think we should go to the igloo. Perhaps Poppy and Joe are there. I have no idea, but it's the only structure in this frozen world." Brett's teeth still chattered as he spoke. The cold weather was bothering him, and he hoped he could warm up in the igloo.

As they walked toward the igloo, Pete said, "It was really cold when we were falling through the hole. I've never been this cold before."

Brett explained that it wasn't a hole in the ground but a portal, and they were most likely now in another time period.

"Really?" Pete was excited. "You mean we could be in the future?"

"Or the past."

"Wow! This is going to make the best article. I could write a feature about time travel and portals. People need to know about this. This will change the entire landscape of the Overworld and our beliefs about time."

Brett chuckled. "I bet this would be interesting to read about, but when you're living it, it's very scary."

"Have you been through a portal before?"

Brett didn't want to go into details about the multiple times he had been in a portal, but he replied, "Yes, a few times. Each time I always wonder if I will make my way back to my own time period. It's missing home that always gets to me."

"That makes sense," said Pete.

As the duo approached the igloo, they saw something walk behind the igloo.

"What was that?" asked Brett. "It looked like a skeleton."

"It's a stray," said Pete. "I wrote an article about them. They are like skeletons, but their arrows are filled with a potion that makes you move a lot slower. Once they have you in their clutches, they destroy you."

"Sounds like a witch," Brett said, and he recalled the many times a witch had thrown a potion on him and then charged toward him, ready to attack.

Brett wailed and grabbed his shoulder, and then he felt as if he couldn't move an inch. "It hit me," Brett mumbled, but his voice sounded like it was in slow motion, and he slurred his words.

Pete took out his diamond sword and hurled it toward the stray, striking the wintery skeleton-like creature with his sword and destroying it. The stray dropped a bone on the ground.

"You're a good fighter," remarked Brett. The arrow's potion had worn off, and he drank a potion of healing to regain his energy.

"Thanks," Pete said. "We have to watch out. There

are probably a lot more strays around, and we don't want to get destroyed. We have to find Poppy and your other friend."

"Joe," Brett said.

"Yes," said Pete.

"We have to go inside the igloo," said Brett.

The duo readjusted their armor before they opened the front door of the igloo. They weren't sure who was living in this icy home or if they were friendly. Brett slowly opened the door and called out, "Is anybody there?"

There was no response, and they walked inside the igloo. The igloo was made of snow blocks, which gave the appearance of the interior being brighter than it was. There weren't many windows, but there was a bed, a furnace, and a crafting table. Brett walked over to the crafting table and perused the blocks on the table. "It looks like someone was crafting a sword."

Pete lifted the floor carpet, and Brett asked, "What are you doing?"

"I'm a reporter that specializes in design. I know all about various structures, and I know that all igloos have a trapdoor under the carpet."

"Really?" Brett questioned. "You write about design?" Brett was disappointed. He was hoping Pete wrote about serious news.

"Yes, that's why I wanted to interview Poppy. She's the best builder in the Overworld. It was a big story for me. Of course, I think I fell"— he laughed —"into a bigger story. I might have to write about something other than design for this article. I mean, we could be in the future."

"Or the past," Brett reminded him.

Pete lifted the lid of the trapdoor. "Do you want to go to the basement with me?"

"Yes." Brett stood by the opening to the basement.

"A few quick tips before we go. The basement has a few snow blocks that are infested."

"Infested? With what?" asked Brett.

Brett didn't know a lot about the cold biome. He had once been asked to build a farm there, and Poppy had constructed an igloo in the cold biome, but he had never studied this region. Brett wasn't a fan of cold weather and did his best to stay in sunny biomes like Meadow Mews. He listened as Pete explained.

"If you break an infested block, you will find that the block is filled with silverfish."

"You have to point those bricks out to me. I don't want to be attacked by those little menacing insects."

"I will," Pete promised.

As they crawled down the ladder to the basement, they heard someone call out, "Help!"

5

IN THE BASEMENT

Brett didn't recognize the voice. He looked over at Pete and said, "We have to help them."

Pete agreed, but added, "I hope this isn't a trap."

Brett pulled a torch from his inventory. The light wasn't that strong, and he couldn't see. "Where are you?"

"Help!" the voice called out again.

"It sounds like they are over there." Pete pointed down a long hall past a brewing station, which was covered in bottles, and a cauldron. Pete warned Brett, "There is usually a cage with a zombie villager in an igloo basement."

Brett didn't like the basement; it creeped him out. It was also colder down in the basement than it was outside. He followed closely behind Pete. He wanted to leave, but he knew he had to help the person crying for help.

"Help!" the voice called out again, but this time it sounded much closer than before.

Pete rushed toward a cage, which housed the person who was calling for help. "Are you okay?" Pete asked.

"No," came the reply. "I was trapped down here."

"Aren't there usually zombie villagers in those cages?" asked Pete as he pried the doors open.

"There was," the person replied, "but I destroyed them. Just when I was about to open the chest in the corner and get my loot, someone pushed me in here and closed the door."

"Who?" asked Pete.

"I have no idea. I didn't have a chance to see their face. I remember they were dressed in blue."

"Dressed in blue!" exclaimed Brett.

"Why? Is that a big deal?" asked the released prisoner.

"Yes," Brett explained. "There were people who were dressed in all blue, and they tried to attack my friend Poppy."

When Brett mentioned Poppy, his heart sunk. He wanted to know where Poppy was, and he wouldn't rest until he found her.

"Thank you for helping me get out," the person said as she pulled a bottle of milk from her inventory. "I was in that cage for weeks. This is my last bottle of milk. I would have starved if you didn't rescue me."

"I'm Pete, and this is Brett."

"I'm Claudia. What were you guys doing down here?"

"Looking for our friends," explained Brett.

"I hope they are okay. It's a grim time in the Overworld," said Claudia.

"It is?" asked Pete.

"Yes, unless you guys haven't been affected by the ice age and the shortage of wheat," she said.

"What?" asked Brett.

"How could you not know about the ice age and the shortage of wheat? You know it's too cold to grow wheat in the other biomes, and people are starving," said Claudia.

Pete said, "The ice age, but that happened . . ." and then he paused. He didn't want Claudia to know they were from the future.

Brett knew a lot about this time period. He had studied the ice age and wheat production when he was learning how to construct a farm in the cold taiga. He also knew they never discovered why it had happened. If they had, it wouldn't have lasted as long and the impact wouldn't have been as devastating. He had no idea how he could stop it, but he wanted to help. However, he had to find his friends first.

Brett said, "I know how to build a farm in the ice."

"You do?" Claudia was impressed. "That could save us. Can we build one now?"

As they made their way out of the igloo, the sun was beginning to set. Brett wondered if building a farm in the icy biome was a good idea. Maybe they should set up a home base and then search for their friends from there. They could craft beds in the igloo, and he could build the farm outside the igloo. He replied, "I think I should build a farm here. I can help us gather wheat, and we can feed the hungry."

"What about Poppy and your friend Joe?" asked Pete, and he added, "And how long do we plan on staying here? Isn't building a farm a lot of work?"

Brett never thought building a farm was work. He enjoyed it so much. He said, "I think this is the only plan that will work. We have to help the people of the Overworld, and if we stay here, we have a better chance of finding our friends. They have to be close by."

Brett was correct. As he spoke, Poppy and Joe came running toward them. Behind Poppy and Joe trailed a couple who were screaming at each other.

"Poppy! Joe!" Brett called out.

Poppy ran to Brett. "When we emerged in this cold biome, these people arrived seconds after us. They are awful," she said in a whisper. "They were at the grand opening, and they accidentally fell into the portal. All they want is to go home. I don't know how I can help them."

"Portal?" Claudia was confused.

"Who are you?" asked Poppy.

"I'm Claudia. I am a treasure hunter. Your friends saved me. I was trapped in a cage," said Claudia.

Brett wanted to mention that a person dressed in blue had trapped Claudia in a cage in the basement of the igloo, but he didn't have a chance to speak. The two people who had fallen through the portal after Poppy and Joe were fighting with each other. Brett walked over to them and said calmly, "Can you speak one at a time? Also, is it possible to lower your voices?"

One of them, a man wearing glasses who introduced himself as Carl, said, "It's getting dark. Is there a place we can stay before we are attacked by hostile mobs?"

"Yes," said his friend, who introduced herself as Alexandra. "We don't want to be attacked."

"We can all stay in the igloo," said Brett. "We just have to craft beds."

The gang followed Brett to the igloo, but as they approached the door, a barrage of arrows struck them. Brett didn't have enough energy to open the door to the igloo because the arrow injected a potion of slowness into his body. Exhaustion set in, and everything felt like it moved in slow motion; it was taking a long time.

"We have to fight back," Pete said.

"I know," Brett said, but instead of leaping at a stray, he let out a yawn.

6
ATTACK OF THE STRAYS

The strays were multiplying as the gang tried to gather enough energy to pull potions from their inventories to help them regain their strength. Everyone was moving in slow motion as the strays made their approach. Brett was able to swing his sword, ripping into the rattling bones of the frozen beast and destroying it.

Night was setting in, and it was hard to see the strays in the darkness, but the strays knew the gang could hear their bones creaking and feel the stings from their arrows. Poppy used her bow and arrow to fight back. She hid behind the side of the igloo and shot arrows at the strays. The only person who was having trouble fighting the strays was Claudia. Her inventory was empty, and she had one heart left. Poppy noticed Claudia moved at a snail's pace and offered her a potion from her inventory.

"Thank you," Claudia said.

As Claudia took a sip, four strays surrounded her. With renewed energy, Claudia struck the strays and destroyed them. One of them dropped an arrow on the ground. Claudia picked it up and handed it to Poppy. "You can have this."

"No, it's yours," said Poppy.

When the final stray was destroyed, the gang rushed into the igloo. Brett suggested they craft beds in the living room near the one bed and the furnace.

"Sounds like a good idea," said Joe. He was tired from his day of time travel and battling the strays and wanted to get to sleep.

"It's a good idea, but it doesn't sound good to me," said Carl.

"Do you want to go outside and be destroyed?" questioned Joe.

"No, he doesn't," Alexandra replied. "We want to go outside and find the portal to get back to the grand opening celebration, but we know it's too dangerous."

"What were you celebrating?" asked Claudia.

"I built a skyscraper, but the celebration was ruined because somebody blew up a few floors of the skyscraper. I hope the rest of the building is okay." Poppy's eyes filled with tears. "I worry that the building is destroyed and I will have to rebuild it."

"That's your biggest concern?" questioned Carl. "Shouldn't you focus on getting back home? I don't want to be here."

"Where are you from?" asked Claudia.

Pete confessed, "We are from the future."

Carl added, "We all fell down a portal and ended up in the past."

Alexandra said, "I didn't even know time travel was possible. I guess we do learn something new every day."

Brett explained, "I know a lot about the ice age and what you guys are going through right now. I read a lot of books about the ice age."

"Reading about it isn't the same as living through it," said Claudia.

"Oh, we know," said Poppy. "We've traveled through time before."

"You have?" Alexandra asked.

"Yeah, a few times," said Joe, "and I know you feel like you will never get back home, but we will get back there."

"You promise?" asked Carl.

Joe wasn't ready to make a promise he wasn't a hundred percent sure he could keep. He replied, "We will try our best."

Alexandra paced the length of the small living room. "We are in the ice age?"

"It's not as bad as you think," said Brett. "We have to get to sleep."

The gang crawled into their beds and tried to sleep. Brett dreamed a million strays were attacking him. The strays surrounded him, and he didn't have anything in his inventory. He had no idea what he was going to do. In the dream, two arrows struck him at once, and he began to move quite slowly. When he called for help, it took ten minutes before he could even get out the entire word. Just as he was about to be destroyed by two strays, he woke up. The sun was melting some of the ice cubes, and he hoped that was a sign the ice age was coming to an end.

Claudia was standing above him. "You mentioned you know how to build a farm in the ice?"

"Yes," he replied. "Joe and I can build it."

Joe said, "But that takes so much time."

"People are starving. We have to help them," said Brett.

Poppy said, "How about you stay here and build the farm, and we work to stop whatever or whomever is causing this ice age?"

Alexandra and Carl were nervous. Carl said, "We don't think we're equipped to stop an ice age. Alexandra and I are just going to search for a portal back to our time period."

Poppy said, "I know this seems scary, but we have to help. There is nothing I want more than to be back in my time period hanging with Joe and Brett and planning pranks. Brett and I are known for our great pranks."

"Is this a prank?" asked Alexandra.

"No, we never pull mean pranks that make people unhappy. We just pull pranks that make people laugh," explained Brett.

Carl said, "I don't think we are going to be helpful. We don't know how to stop an ice age."

"Neither do we," said Poppy, "but we will figure out how we can help."

Brett said, "I've read tons of history books about the ice age, and I know that it just stopped and the weather became warmer. Nobody knew what caused it."

"If we stop it earlier," said Joe, "we could save a lot of people."

"How did it start?" asked Pete. "Were there any warning signs?"

"No," Claudia and Brett answered in unison.

Claudia said, "One day we woke up and it was bitter cold, and all of our crops were destroyed."

Poppy remarked, "You must be so hungry."

"I am," said Claudia.

Everyone in the room grabbed food from their inventories and handed it to Claudia. Poppy said, "Today you will feast."

Claudia smiled as she thanked everyone for their generous offerings. "I feel like I will never be hungry again."

Alexandra looked at Claudia and said, "We will help you. We will try our best to solve this problem and stop the ice age."

A cold wind pushed the igloo door open. Brett looked outside and saw someone dressed in blue in the distance. He hurried outside, but there wasn't anybody there.

7
THE HUNGER

"Brett?" Poppy ran after him and asked, "What's the matter?"

"It was just the wind," said Joe. "That's why the door opened."

"I thought I saw someone dressed in blue," said Brett.

"Blue?" Claudia asked. "Like the person who trapped me in the cage!"

"You were trapped by a person in blue?" asked Poppy.

"Yes," Claudia replied, "but I didn't see what their face looked like."

"I think we found a connection," said Poppy. "I want to find these people in blue and see if they are behind this ice age and famine."

Brett stayed behind and worked on the farm with Joe as Poppy left with Pete, Claudia, Carl, and

Alexandra to find out who was causing the frozen era. Brett was crafting the farm when he heard a noise in the distance.

"Do you hear that?" he asked Joe.

Joe listened. "Does it sound like people talking?"

"Yes," said Brett, and they left the farm to see who was around, but after walking for a while, they found no one except a large polar bear.

"Watch out," Joe warned as the polar bear approached them and began to move its back legs. It leaped at Brett. They had gotten too close to the bear, and it was ready to annihilate them.

"Ouch!" Brett wailed in pain. The bear had him trapped, and he knew he was about to be mauled by this massive bear.

Joe grabbed his bow and arrow and shot a succession of arrows at the bear. The enormous white bear cried in pain and was destroyed. Joe picked up the raw salmon the bear had dropped.

"I will never get used to the cold biome," said Brett as he drank a potion of healing and walked back to the farm.

"I wonder where the people are. It's odd that we both heard voices, but nobody was there," said Joe.

They didn't hear anything as they worked on the farm. Both of them had spent a long time studying how to construct a farm in the cold, and they knew they had limited supplies, but they worked hard as they took out their torches and used them to melt the ice.

Meanwhile Poppy was trekking through the

Overworld with her new friends. They had reached the first village, and Poppy was shocked to see the devastation. People were walking around like zombies. They had no food, and the land outside of the town was barren.

Carl and Alexandra bickered the entire time, and Claudia told them to conserve their energy because fighting was going to exhaust them. "Soon you will see how it feels to live a life of hunger."

"A life of hunger," repeated Pete. "That seems like a great title for an article. I have to chronicle the world of the hungry."

Once Pete had this idea for an article, he wanted to stop every person they met and ask them how they felt. After he did this to two people, Poppy said, "Pete, I know you're a journalist, but this isn't the time to ask people how they are reacting to their situation. You should be trying to find out who is behind this attack on the Overworld."

Pete didn't listen to Poppy. A person from the town asked them if they were lost, and Pete responded by asking them how they were dealing with the feeling of being hungry all the time.

"It's awful," the townsperson replied, "but don't you feel the same way? Or do you know a way to get us food?"

"No," replied Pete, "I don't have a way of getting us food. Although my friends are constructing a farm in the icy biome next to your town."

"They know how to build a farm in the ice?" The

townsperson was impressed and asked, "Can we go there? I miss eating apples."

"I never liked apples," said Carl.

"How can you say that? Can't you see how much this person misses apples?" asked Alexandra.

Carl and Alexandra began to fight about apples, and Claudia once again reminded them to conserve their energy.

"I think they like fighting, and I don't think they're going to stop. I have been with them since we arrived here, and they haven't taken a break from fighting," said Poppy.

"I don't know how I am going to deal with it," said Claudia.

"It's too much," agreed Pete, and then he asked them politely, "Carl and Alexandra, can you please take a break? We understand you both have opinions on apples, but this isn't the best time to discuss it."

Claudia spotted a person dressed in blue running in the distance, and she raced toward them. Poppy followed Claudia, and they both approached the person.

"Hi," Claudia said awkwardly, because she didn't know how to ask this stranger why they were dressed all in blue and if they happened to be associated with the people who had trapped her in the cage.

"Hi," the woman in blue said and asked, "Do I know you?"

"No," Claudia said. "We are new to this town, and we need a place to stay. Do you know of any?"

"No," the woman replied. "And why would you

want to stay here? This town is suffering. We have no resources here. The blacksmith closed up shop because we have no resources to trade. The library even closed because nobody could be bothered to read books anymore. This is a ghost town. You could probably stay in one of the many empty houses because nobody wants to stay here anymore. It's odd that you came here and want to stay. If I were you, I'd leave."

"Can you lead us to an empty house?" asked Claudia.

"If you walk outside of the village, you will find one. In fact, most of them are empty. You'll see there is nothing in them. People took whatever they had, which wasn't much," said the woman, and then she asked, "Do you have anything in your inventory that I can eat?"

Poppy pulled out an apple. "An apple! I haven't seen one of these in ages," the woman said fervently.

Another townsperson heard the word apple and hurried over. "An apple? How did you get that? Apples haven't grown in the Overworld in ages."

"I saved them," said Poppy.

"And you're kind enough to share them with a stranger?" asked the townsperson.

"Yes," she said.

"I want one too," the townsperson demanded.

"You aren't very polite," said Poppy.

"Okay, I want one too, please," said the townsperson.

Poppy went to grab an apple from her inventory, but she didn't have any left. "I'm sorry, that was my last apple."

The townsperson grabbed the apple from the woman who was dressed in blue. She screamed, "That's my apple."

The townsperson didn't care. He pulled the apple from her hand and took a bite. The woman grabbed the apple from his hand and took a big bite. Apple chunks spit from his mouth as he yelled at her to give the apple back.

Poppy yelled, "Stop it! Stop fighting over an apple. I know you guys are hungry, but you can't act like this. If you do, we will never solve the problem of everything being frozen."

The townsperson laughed. "Solve this? How?"

"We have to figure out how to make the Overworld warmer so it will be a hospitable environment and crops can grow again," said Poppy.

"That sounds like a great idea, but it's never going to happen," said the townsperson.

"We will solve it," said Poppy.

"I think you're wasting your time," said the townsperson.

"Well, we have to try," said Poppy.

"We don't even know how it all began," said the townsperson.

Everyone was surprised when the woman in blue said, "I think I know how it started."

8
DISPLACED

"You do?" asked Claudia.

"I'm not sure," the woman replied and then said, "You know what, I don't know how it started."

Pete spit a bunch of questions at the woman, "Why did you change your mind? Are there reasons for that?"

Alexandra and Carl were fighting, but they stopped when they heard Pete blast the woman with a barrage of questions. They added one to the list. "Hey," said Carl, "what's your name?"

Alexandra questioned, "Who are you?"

The woman in blue walked away. As she did she said, "My name is Cara. I'm displaced. I used to live in a town, but now I have no home."

Poppy hurried toward the woman. "I'm sorry to hear this, but we need to know any information you have about the ice age because we must stop it and save the people of the Overworld."

Cara paused. "I live in a town where we are all forced to wear blue. It wasn't always like that. There was once a time when we were able to pick out our own skins."

"Who is making you dress in blue?" asked Poppy.

"Anya," said the woman. "She is the head of our town, although nobody voted her into that position. She showed up one day and demanded we all wear blue. She is a fan of the cold weather, and I think she manipulated this weather situation, but I'm not sure how."

"Can you please take me to your town?" asked Poppy.

"I escaped from that town. I don't want to go back," said Cara.

"We will go with you," Poppy told her.

"I don't want to go back. I'm sorry, I can't." She looked at Poppy, and her eyes were filled with tears.

Pete was standing close by and listening and suggested, "Why don't you tell us where you are from, and we will travel there."

Cara's eyes brightened as she pulled out a map. "It's not far from here." She pointed to the map. "You have to go through the swamp and then over this large hill, and you will find a town that is over the mountain. You will know you are there because everyone dresses in blue. Also, everyone is a builder. There is a lot of construction going on there. When I left, we were all working together to build a castle for Anya."

Poppy took the map. "Thank you," she said to Cara. "We will go and try to solve this crisis."

"Thank you," Cara said softly as she walked away.

Alexandra and Carl jogged toward Poppy and looked at the map. "Seriously?" asked Alexandra. "We have to climb up a mountain? I hate climbing."

Carl said, "I hate swamps. You know how I feel about witches."

"I don't like witches, but it's something we have to do to save the Overworld," explained Poppy.

Pete was the only one who was excited about the trip. "The story is unfolding," he said with a smile. "I bet we will expose who is behind this ice, and I will have an award-winning article."

Poppy laughed. "Pete, do you only care about the story?"

"No," Pete explained. "I do care about saving the Overworld, but I also think it's important to keep a record and have an article where people could learn the facts."

Poppy couldn't debate that comment, so she just looked at the map and led them into the swamp.

Claudia was the first person to point out a hostile mob in the swampy biome. She had stopped by the murky water when she watched a bat fly overhead and said, "I think I hear something."

"What is it?" asked Poppy.

Boing! Boing! Boing!

"It sounds like slimes," said Claudia.

The gang listened to the sound of bouncing slimy mobs, and within seconds they were confronted with the creatures. They used their swords to destroy the beasts, but the slimes weren't easy to defeat. They broke into smaller slimes, and it seemed as if this battle against the slimes might be never-ending.

As they destroyed the final slime, the sun started to set. "Should we stay here?" Poppy asked the group.

"Stay here?" Alexandra's shrill voice screamed. "No way."

"You have to speak softly," Carl yelled. "You don't want a witch to hear us."

"You are also yelling," Claudia reminded them in a soft voice. "We all have to calm down and figure out where we should build a structure. It isn't safe being outside at night, and we want to conserve our energy. Once you go through your food in your inventory, you will begin to understand how it feels to be hungry. I promise you, it's awful, and you don't want to feel that way. Please work together to solve this problem, and then we can all eat again. We can't waste our energy fighting."

Poppy had already taken a bunch of supplies from her inventory and started constructing a house by the water. "We are staying here," she said as she built the foundation for one side of the house.

Everyone took out whatever supplies they had to help Poppy build the house. They were putting the windows on the house when they heard laughter in the distance.

"That sounds like a witch." Carl's voice cracked when he spoke.

"It does," Claudia said, "but we can't get upset about

the witch. We have to find her and battle her. I don't have any potions left in my inventory, but I do have a diamond sword. If someone wants to splash a potion on her, I will strike her with my diamond sword."

Pete pulled a potion out. "Come with me, Claudia," he called out as he sprinted toward the sound of the witch.

The witch's hut was in the middle of the swamp. The purple-robed witch charged toward them clutching a potion in one hand, but Pete skillfully splashed a potion on the witch as Claudia struck her with her diamond sword. The duo destroyed the witch in record time.

"We make a good team," said Claudia.

Pete was about to respond when a second witch darted out of the hut and splashed Claudia. "Help," Claudia said faintly. The witch had left Claudia with one heart.

Pete swung his sword with one hand and splashed a potion with his other hand and defeated the second witch. He rushed toward Claudia with a potion for healing. As she took a sip, they heard their friends cry out in the distance, "Help!"

9
FARM OR FAMINE

Claudia and Pete rushed toward their friends, making their way through the dark swamp where the only light came from the large full moon in the sky. They were almost at the house when they saw their friends battling chunks of slime. Slimes surrounded Poppy, Alexandra, and Carl, and they were losing hearts fast.

"We have to help them," Pete shouted as he raced toward the slimes, still clutching his potion in one hand and his sword in the other. Pete splashed a potion on the slimes and slashed them with his sword. When the final slime was defeated, the gang hurried into the newly constructed house and crafted beds.

Poppy could barely keep her eyes open. "I hope we make some discoveries tomorrow," she said with a yawn.

"Me too," said Pete.

"I am really nervous about climbing over the mountain," said Alexandra. "I hate heights. In fact, I'm outright scared of them."

"We will be beside you," said Carl, "and will help you."

Poppy was surprised Carl had said something so comforting to Alexandra. Since she had met them, all she ever heard was their yelling at each other. It was nice to see that they were sometimes kind too.

Poppy closed her eyes and dreamed about being back in her time period. She dreamed about the grand opening. In her dream, everything went according to plan. The crowd was pleased to see the new building, and everyone marveled at the rooftop farm. When Poppy woke up, she was thinking about Brett and Joe. She hoped they were making progress on the icy farm.

Meanwhile in the icy cold biome, Brett didn't dream that night. He was too tired because he had spent all day working on the farm, and the intensity of the labor exhausted him. Brett had never felt so tired in his entire life. When he crawled into bed, he looked over at Joe, but his friend was already snoring. Brett didn't know if they would be able to create enough wheat to help the people of the Overworld. The famine had lasted a long time, and he was kidding himself if he felt he could solve it by creating one farm. When he woke up, refreshed from a night of sleep, he came up with an idea.

"We are going to teach people how to farm in the ice," Brett announced.

"We are?" asked Joe.

"Yes." Brett paced around the igloo as he talked. "This will become a school. We will invite people from across the Overworld to learn how to farm. They can all go back to their lands and teach others."

"That sounds like an awesome idea," said Joe.

"But how are we going to tell everyone about it?" asked Brett. "We have to finish it first and then travel the Overworld to tell people about the school."

"We should see what the farm looks like today," said Joe. "We still haven't grown anything yet, and we have to evaluate how long it will take before the farm is functional."

Brett agreed, and the duo jogged out of the igloo to the farm. When they arrived at the farm, Joe screamed, "Oh no!"

The farm was destroyed. Someone had pulled out everything they had planted and frozen everything so nothing could grow. All of their hard work was a waste of time. Brett began to cry. Joe said, "We will find out who did this."

Brett questioned, "How come we didn't hear anyone? It doesn't make sense. We were just in the igloo next to the farm." As Brett spoke, he realized that they had been fast asleep that night. An explosion wouldn't have woken them up — they were that tired.

Joe began to clean up the mess and pulled out a torch from his inventory to melt the ice that had formed over their wheat. "We can't get upset about this. We just have to move forward."

Brett joined Joe, and they worked together to rebuild the farm. As they melted all the ice, they heard people talking in the distance. Brett and Joe quietly went to investigate. As they hid behind the igloo, they could see a man and a woman dressed in all blue. The people approached the igloo, and Brett and Joe ran to the other side of it. They could hear the people in blue talking as they entered the igloo.

"It looks like we scared those people off," said the man.

"I know." The woman laughed. "Why did they even bother trying to make a farm in the ice? It's so much easier to build it underground like Anya does."

"There's nothing in this igloo," said the man. "Let's go."

Brett and Joe leaped at the people when they exited the igloo. Brett slammed his sword into the woman's unarmored blue shirt. "You destroyed our farm."

Brett could hear her say, "I'm sorry," before she was destroyed.

Joe obliterated the man with one hit from his sword. Joe's voice was tinged with guilt when he said, "They were surprised. They had no way to defend themselves."

"They destroyed our farm," said Brett, but even he felt guilty. He had heard the woman say she was sorry.

Joe said, "I think we should find Poppy and the others. I think once we find out who Anya is and if she is behind this attack on the Overworld, we will be able to stop the ice age."

"I agree," said Brett, "but where should we look for them?"

"I don't know," said Joe.

Brett and Joe stared at the miles of icy landscape that stretched in front of them. They weren't sure where they were going, but they knew they had to go.

10

SKINS

Pete looked at the hill and said, "Alexandra, you will make it over, and you will help us find out what is going on in this town."

"I'm going to try," said Alexandra as she started to climb.

They walked slowly until they reached the top, and then Carl held Alexandra's hand and said, "Alexandra, take a deep breath and look at the view."

Alexandra's eyes were closed. "I can't. I just can't."

Claudia said, "Alexandra, we are here beside you. You will love the view. It's stunning, and you deserve to see it because you made it this far."

Alexandra opened one eye and marveled at the verdant landscape but noted the thin layer of ice that was atop the grass. "This would be a much nicer view if the grass wasn't covered in ice. We have to stop this ice age." And she bravely took a step down the hill and toward the village, where the people in blue lived.

When they reached the bottom of the hill, Poppy pulled out the map and studied it. "It looks like the town is in this direction." She pointed toward a large meadow.

The gang walked for what seemed like an eternity, and they were beginning to lose hope.

"Are you sure we are going in the right direction?" asked Pete.

"I'm not," confessed Poppy as she stared at Cara's map.

"Should we have trusted Cara?" questioned Carl.

"It's too late now. We already followed her directions," said Alexandra.

As they looked at the map, they heard a voice call out.

"Guys!"

The gang turned around to see Cara. "I changed my mind," she said as she caught her breath. "I can lead you there."

"What made you change your mind?" Pete asked.

"I have to confront Anya. She destroyed my town, and I want to know why," said Cara.

The group trekked through the icy grass and headed to a small town that reminded them of Meadow Mews. The minute Cara stepped into the village, a neighbor recognized her.

"Cara," the neighbor dressed in blue asked, "where have you been?"

"I've been looking for a town that had more resources and food, but I wasn't able to find one," explained Cara.

"You should have stayed here. Anya built an underground farm, and if you are a good citizen, she will let you take an apple."

"How does she decide if you are good or not?" asked Pete.

"Who are you?" the neighbor asked.

Cara said, "These are my friends. They are coming to stay with me for a while. I met them while I was traveling."

The neighbor looked at the gang and shook her head. "You guys can't stay here unless you change your skins. Anya would not approve."

"Do we have to change them?" asked Poppy. "I like my skin."

"If you don't change, I will have to report you."

"You will?" asked Carl. "Why do you have to tell on us?"

The neighbor explained, "If I don't, Anya won't give me my weekly apple."

"She only lets you have an apple once a week?" Cara was infuriated. She signaled for the group to follow her, and she said goodbye to her neighbor. As they walked toward her house, other neighbors called out to her, but she didn't respond. She didn't want to be lectured about her new friends' skins and how they must change them to make Anya happy.

Cara thought about how pleasant her town was

before Anya arrived. It was a small town where everyone was friendly and shared the wealth of goods from their farms. Now she lived in a town where her neighbor was about to report her for having friends that looked different from everyone else. She had to stop Anya. As they approached her house, Cara was shocked to see four people blocking the entranceway to her home.

"What is going on here?" asked Cara.

"You must report to Anya," one of the people said.

Pete wouldn't admit this to any of his friends, but he was excited to meet the leader. He had imagined that it would have taken them a long time to meet the person who controlled the town. He believed that once he met her, the gang would be able to overthrow her and order would be restored to the Overworld.

They followed the blue soldiers to a large castle. As they walked through the town, Poppy noted all of the construction that was taking place. Anya must have ordered all sorts of buildings to be built. There seemed to be no order to their placement. There were bridges that led to nowhere and large wooden boats, but there was no water in sight. There were also multiple barns, but she didn't see any animals.

The castle was one of the few buildings that seemed to be in use. Cara whispered to the gang, "This is where Anya lives. She forced the entire town to build it for her."

The gang was led past a row of guards and into the castle. Claudia said, "I've never been in a place this grand," but she also whispered to her friends, "I'm scared. A person in blue trapped me in a cage, and I hope they don't trap us here."

"A person in blue tried to force me out of the skyscraper I was building. I'm also worried," said Poppy.

They walked into a large room where a woman dressed in blue sat on a throne.

"Poppy," the woman said, "I'm so glad to finally meet you. I'm Anya."

Poppy stood silently and stared at Anya.

Anya said, "I like that you made it here on your own. It is as if we were destined to meet."

"So you were behind the attack in Meadow Mews. I spent so long building that skyscraper. Why did you attack it?"

"The skyscraper is fine," Anya reassured her. "I wanted you to come here and build something for me. Now that you are here, I want you to start today."

"Today? What do you want me to build?"

"A skyscraper, but a larger one than you had in your time period. I want my town to have the first skyscraper, and I want it to be massive."

"What if I refuse?" asked Poppy.

"Nonsense," said Anya. "But before we start anything, every one of you has to change their skin. We only wear blue in this town."

"We don't want to stay," announced Poppy.

"You don't have a choice," said Anya.

Poppy fled from the castle, but she stopped when she heard a familiar voice call out, "Please listen to her."

Poppy turned around and saw Brett and Joe being held captive by Anya's soldiers. One of them had a sword against Brett's chest. Poppy walked back to Anya.

11
REUNION

Brett and Joe had stumbled upon the town by accident. They didn't have a map, but they did have a plan. They wanted to stop the ice age. Brett thought he'd warm up once he left the icy biome, but even when they reached a small seaside town, he noticed a layer of ice on the sand.

"You don't realize how awful the ice age is until you see frozen sand," remarked Joe. "This is the beach. People should be sunbathing, but it's empty, as if the sun is broken."

Brett looked up at the sun. "In the history books, they talk about this time as the great darkness. They also say that one day it just miraculously ended and the Overworld was warm again and all the crops grew and flowers bloomed."

"I know," said Joe. "I always thought it was a strange explanation."

The sun was beginning to set as they made their way inland and found themselves walking through a village street. Joe pointed out that everyone in the town was dressed in blue.

Brett said, "This is a good sign. This means we are closer to discovering the reason for the ice age. We know these people in blue have to have some answers."

"We need to find Anya," said Joe.

"That will probably be harder than we think," warned Brett.

The duo, dressed in their own skins, stood out in the town. When they reached the butcher shop that was shuttered, someone called out to them.

"Strangers!" the voice boomed.

Crowds surrounded Brett and Joe, and they were nervous. They didn't want to be attacked. "We don't want to hurt anyone," said Brett.

"I'm Joe, and this is my friend Brett," Joe announced to the group, but the group wasn't happy with their introductions.

"We need to take you to get your skin changed." A man dressed in blue held a sword against Brett's back, and another pointed a sword at Joe. They marched the pair to the castle.

When Brett and Joe arrived in the castle, they were taken to meet Anya. She sat on the throne and said, "You have appeared in my town. We haven't had any new people in the town for a while. Now that you are here, you must change your skin. Once the change has been completed, you will be a resident of my town and will never leave."

"Never leave?" asked Brett.

"Why does this bother you?" questioned Anya.

"I want to go home," replied Brett.

"Me too," added Joe.

"There's no need to go home. This is your home now," said Anya.

Brett didn't want to fight. He knew it was pointless. He had to save his energy and plan his escape. He followed the soldiers to the room where he was to change his skin. As he entered, he realized he couldn't undergo this procedure. He didn't want to give up his identity. He swiftly pulled out his diamond sword and swung it at the soldier. Joe also slammed his sword into the other soldier. When word got out about this uprising, Anya ordered more soldiers to stop the attack. The soldiers swung their swords at the duo until both Brett and Joe each had one heart left. Then the soldiers marched them in to see Anya.

Brett was shocked to see Poppy, Claudia, Pete, Alexandra, and Carl standing before Anya. He didn't want his friends to suffer a fate like his. He called out, "Please listen to her." By saying these four words, Brett believed that Anya would lead them all to the changing room, and then they could revolt. Now that he had his friends with him, he knew they wouldn't be as easy to defeat.

Poppy was shocked and relieved to see her two good friends. The minute she saw them, she was reminded of all the good times she had shared with Brett. She wished she could be back in Meadow Mews pulling pranks on their friends Helen and Nancy. She didn't want to be here, trapped in a frozen castle. She knew she had to fight to get back home.

Poppy said, "We will listen to you. We will change our skins."

Once Poppy said these words, she was reunited with her friends Joe and Brett. They were all marched to the changing room. As they waited to get the skins that were picked out for them, Poppy splashed a potion of invisibility on herself, ordered her friends to do the same, and said, "Meet in the Nether." Claudia didn't have a potion, so Joe splashed some on her. Soon the gang was invisible, but they didn't have a plan on where they were going to build the Nether portal.

Poppy bolted out of the castle and ran as fast and far as she could until she emerged in a grassy meadow. She placed obsidian on the icy grass. As she placed the first piece, she noticed that her hand came into focus. She looked over to her right and saw Joe standing with another piece of obsidian. Within seconds all of her friends reemerged in front of her.

"I love happy endings." She smiled.

"But this isn't one." Joe pointed at the army sprinting toward them. The gang tried to build the portal as fast as they could, but time was running out.

12

NETHER MEANT TO HURT YOU

"Hurry!" Poppy said as they rushed to craft the portal.

"Why are we going to the Nether?" asked Carl.

"I hate the Nether," said Alexandra.

"Everyone does," Poppy said, "and we don't have time to discuss it now. We just have to get to the Nether. I have a plan."

The blue army was advancing, and the gang feared they wouldn't be able to ignite the portal in time. They kept close together as they stood on the portal waiting for it to work, and soon the purple smoke enveloped them. They were relieved when they emerged in the Nether.

"The heat feels good," said Brett. He had forgotten what it felt like to feel warm. Sweat formed on his brow as he explored the lava river behind him.

"What's the plan?" asked Claudia.

"I wanted Anya's army to follow us here and for us to battle them in the Nether. It was the only way we could escape. If we stayed in the Overworld, they would defeat us. They have too much power there. We all have the same amount of power in the Nether."

Brett said, "I like that idea, but I thought you had a more detailed plan."

Poppy asked, "Can you come up with a better one? When I found you guys, you were trapped in Anya's castle."

Brett admitted he didn't have another plan. He thought about his idea of creating a school to teach people how to farm in the ice. He liked the idea of teaching people how to farm, and perhaps if he made it back to his time period, he might consider starting a farming school, but it wasn't a great plan in their current situation. They needed a plan that would stop Anya from destroying the Overworld.

The gang didn't have time to come up with an intricate plan. Within seconds, the blue army emerged in the Nether and sprinted toward them. They were in the middle of battling the blue army when another batch of soldiers arrived in the Nether.

"There are too many of them," Alexandra said as she struck a soldier in blue. She was down to two hearts and was exhausted.

As Poppy slammed her sword into another soldier, she realized her plan wasn't that good. They had to find another way to get rid of Anya.

Pete came up with an idea. As he struck a blue

soldier, the soldier begged him to stop, and Pete listened. "I don't want to hurt you," Pete said, "but you guys are leaving me with no choice. I have to defend myself."

The blue soldier shocked Pete when he said, "I am not going to attack you anymore. There is no reason to defend yourself."

Pete wasn't sure if this was a trick. He looked around and saw all of his friends battling blue soldiers, and he wondered why his soldier had chosen to end the battle.

"Why?" Pete asked.

"This isn't my battle. I am not going to destroy myself for Anya. She forced me to change my skin, and because of her and her command blocks, we are living in an inhospitable environment."

"Command blocks?" asked Pete.

"Yes, she has them set up in the basement of the castle. That is how she is controlling the temperature of the Overworld."

Pete said, "We have to stop her."

"I would love to, but how?" asked the soldier.

Pete said, "Please call out to your friends and have them stop battling us."

The blue soldier called out, "Stop!" His voice was so loud, it created a wave in the lava river.

The sound of his voice made everyone put down their weapons. One soldier called out, "What's the matter?"

Poppy and the others pointed their swords at the blue soldier. Pete told them to back off. As Pete said those words, the soldiers started to advance toward the lone blue soldier.

The blue soldier said, "Destroy me if you must, but please let me speak first." The soldiers backed away, and he spoke. "I don't want to battle these people because they have the same dream I do. They want to stop the ice age. I don't want Anya controlling me. If you agree with me, please put down your swords, and I will tell you my plan to save the Overworld."

Everybody put down their swords.

"I want to go back to Anya and act as if we captured these people. Once we get there, I want to overthrow the castle. I want to break the command blocks and end the ice age. I want to go back to wearing my old skin."

The soldier was shocked when the crowd cheered him on. "We want our old skins back too!"

Poppy marveled at this turn of events. She didn't imagine this happening at all, and she looked over at Pete and smiled.

Pete and Brett didn't trust this turn of events. It seemed too easy, and they wished there was a way these soldiers could prove their loyalty to this idea. Their wish was granted when a group of ghasts swooped down and began to attack the group with fireballs. The gang had to fight back together.

Brett aimed his bow and arrow at a ghast. Then he tripped and was about to fall into the lava waterfall until one of the soldiers helped him avoid splashing into the lethal lava. Brett realized they were all working together, and soon they would stop Anya.

The soldier had finished lecturing everyone on his plan. They were to hop on the portal and show Anya how they had captured these rebels and would take them to the changing room. Once they made that announcement and she was happy, they would stage their surprise attack.

Everyone agreed they had to attack Anya, and they huddled together on the portal. They hoped it was going to work. As they emerged in the cold Overworld, they shivered.

The blue soldier walked into Anya's castle and announced, "We got them."

"Good job," said Anya.

"Thank you," the soldier said and smiled.

Anya lectured the group, "You tried to escape. You know there will be a punishment for this. But first you must change into your new skins. I know you don't want to and you feel as if you were defeated, but I assure you that once you are in your new skin, you will be much happier."

"They will be," said the blue soldier.

"I know," said Anya. "This is the center of the Overworld, and they will be involved in changing history." She pointed at Poppy. "You will start constructing the building first thing in the morning."

"She will create a stunning skyscraper," said the blue soldier.

"Of course she will. Now lead them to the changing room," she ordered.

As they walked down the hall toward the room, the

soldier didn't attack Anya or any other soldier there. The other soldiers that followed behind seemed confused. They were waiting for the soldier to follow their plan, but as the gang walked into the changing room and picked out their new skins, they wondered if they had been tricked.

13
FOLLOWERS

Brett thought about the soldier who had helped him when he was about to slip into the lava lake. He trusted these people. How could they have turned on them? Brett had chosen his skin when the soldier said, "Are you ready? Then we will attack?"

Brett said, "We are fighting in new skins?"

"What?" Poppy was confused.

"Yes," the blue soldier responded. "We all have to look the same. Once we defeat Anya, we can all go back to our old skins. I remember mine. I wore an orange shirt and yellow pants. I can't wait to wear them again."

Having them all change skins to battle Anya made sense, but Brett felt giving up his skin for a battle was a hard sacrifice to make. He liked wearing his old skin because it was the one he had chosen ages ago, and he felt comfortable in it. He also feared that once he changed into the skin the soldiers would turn on him and he'd be trapped wearing blue pants and a blue shirt forever in a cold world.

Claudia was the first to change her skin, followed by Alexandra and Carl, but before Poppy, Joe, Pete, and Brett could get their skins changed, the uprising had begun. An impatient blue soldier lunged toward Anya and slammed his sword into her, taking her by surprise.

"Stop!" Anya shouted and called for more troops.

Blue soldiers stormed into Anya's room and looked for her attacker, but they couldn't find them. Since everyone was dressed the same, they had no idea who was the one who had tried to overthrow Anya.

The attacker snuck behind Anya and struck her again. "Stop!" she called out, but nobody had been looking when the soldier had quietly made his way toward Anya, and again they had no idea who had attacked her.

Anya had one heart left. She went to pull a glass of milk from her inventory, but it was empty. She didn't want them to know she had an empty inventory. It had been a long time since she had to acquire items. She was used to people bringing things to her, and she was rusty both in keeping her inventory stocked and in battle. She couldn't admit this, so she ordered everyone, "Get in one line. I want to meet with each of you and find out who is attacking me. You will be found, and you won't get away with this."

The blue soldiers listened. They stood in a single-file line, and Anya walked up and down staring at each soldier. After walking up and down the line a few times, she realized that she had no idea who was behind this attack, and she had to find another plan.

"Where are the new people? Where is Poppy?" Anya questioned the crowd.

"They have changed their skins. You told us to bring them to the changing room," replied the blue soldier.

Anya realized her mistake. Now she had no idea who Poppy and the others were, and they could attack her at any minute. In the past, she didn't care about the soldiers' individual traits, but now she needed to know who the newcomers were and if they were the ones who were attacking her.

Anya announced, "I want everyone to go back to their old skins immediately," as she marched them all to the changing room.

Anya was the only one who didn't need to change into her old skin. She was wearing her original skin, which was a dark blue shirt and pants. The soldiers wore the same outfit in a shade of lighter blue. Anya watched as the soldiers emerged from the room in their normal skins, but as she stood watching the rows of soldiers transform, she didn't realize people were lurking behind her. She felt something press against her back.

"Don't move," said Brett.

"I won't," Anya said. She only had one heart left, and she didn't want to be destroyed.

"You will lead us to the command blocks," ordered Brett.

Anya replied, "Okay."

"Now," Brett said.

Anya turned around to see Brett, Poppy, and their friends dressed in their old skins.

"You were never dressed like the soldiers?" she asked.

"No," replied Poppy.

"Then who was attacking me?" asked Anya, but as she said those words, she knew she didn't want a response because she dreaded the answer. It was her own people and that meant that she would no longer be able to rule her cold town. However, she wasn't going to give up without a fight. There were definitely people who believed in her cold way of life, and they would defend her.

The gang marched her toward the room that held the command blocks; then they heard screams. A group of people didn't want to change their skins from their blue soldier uniforms. Anya knew she had loyal followers, and she knew her battle wasn't over. It had just begun.

14
MOB INVASION

Three people remained in blue skins. Anya wished more people would have stayed with her, but she was glad she had this army of three. They could help her escape and stop these intruders from destroying the command blocks. She stood by the door where she housed the command blocks. She only had one heart left, but the three soldiers charged toward Anya and blocked everyone from attacking her. One of the blue soldiers handed her a potion of healing, which she gulped down.

"Stand back!" she ordered, but nobody listened. The three soldiers were no match for the dozens of attackers.

Poppy hurtled toward Anya and called out to the crowd, "Stop!"

Anya was surprised. "What are you doing? Have you finally come to your senses and joined me?"

Poppy asked, "Why are you doing this? Why would you make the Overworld freeze?"

Anya didn't respond.

"Answer her!" Brett called out.

Anya was about to speak when she cried out in pain. An arrow shot through her arm, and then another arrow hit her leg.

Skeletons spawned in the castle. During the battle, the sun had set and it was night. They weren't prepared for the hostile mob attack. A spider jockey stood at the entrance to the castle and was about to make its way in. Anya used this opportunity to escape. She sped out of the castle with the three soldiers. The gang wanted to fight her, but they couldn't because they were under attack from the skeleton army and the spider jockey.

Alexandra and Carl fought the spider jockey. They worked together and aimed their bow and arrows at the skeleton atop the red-eyed spider. Their arrows destroyed the skeleton, and then they both traded in their bow and arrows for swords. They collectively slammed their swords into the spider, destroying it.

More skeletons filled the castle, and the group was exhausted from battling the bony beasts. It seemed as if once they destroyed a skeleton, another would spawn in its place. The battle seemed pointless and never-ending. It became more complicated when a cluster of vacant-eyed zombies lumbered toward the castle door. The smell of rotten flesh overwhelmed the group, and they tried to hold their breath as they battled the undead beasts.

"We have to find Anya," said Poppy.

"I know," replied Brett, but he knew they had to destroy these hostile mobs before they could leave. Also it probably wasn't a good idea to travel at night. There were more hostile mobs, and if the group used their remaining resources battling them, they wouldn't be able to fight Anya.

When the final skeleton and zombie were destroyed, Poppy said again, "We have to find Poppy."

"In the morning," said Brett. "It's dark, and we need to rest."

"Where will we stay?" asked Poppy.

"You can stay at my house," said Cara.

The gang followed Cara as they hurried through the cold town in the dark. Cara led them to a large glass house.

"You built this?" asked Poppy.

"Yes," said Cara, "years ago."

Poppy was impressed with the design. "I've built a glass house before, but this one is incredible."

"This isn't the time to talk about building," Brett reminded her. "We have to get to bed."

Cara offered her guests any room in the house. There were multiple rooms, and there was enough space for everyone. Brett chose a room off the living room. He climbed into a bed and looked out the window of the glass house and could see the entire town. He didn't see any hostile mobs, and he closed his eyes and went to bed. He dreamed about Anya. He saw her show up in the glass house and order them to leave. She had replenished her army, and they were stronger than before. When he woke up, the sun was blazing through the window of the house. Brett touched his head, and sweat was on his fingers. He felt hot.

Brett hurried out of his room to find Pete writing in a notebook. Pete said, “Good morning. I’m getting so many notes for this article. Nobody is going to believe that I saw a piece of history and was able to time travel. This article is going to win an award.”

“Pete,” Brett asked, “do you feel hot?”

Pete stopped for a moment. “I do!” he exclaimed. “I feel hot.”

“I think someone has destroyed the command blocks,” said Brett.

Poppy and the others rushed into the living room and announced, “I think the ice age is over.”

Cara said, “We have to go to the castle. I bet the townspeople have taken control of it and have broken the command blocks.”

“I hope they trapped Anya,” said Carl.

“Me too,” said Alexandra.

A rush of cold air blew through the room and the front door opened. A voice boomed through the living room. “Don’t get your hopes up. I’m not trapped,” said Anya.

Behind Anya was a large group of people dressed in blue. It was just like Brett’s dream, but this was something he couldn’t wake up from.

15

MISSING HISTORY

"It's time to surrender," Anya announced to the group.

Brett was battling the army, but the frigid air that blew through the living room distracted him. Had the command blocks been destroyed and then rebuilt? Or did the house just feel warm because of the direct sunlight coming through the windows? All of these questions swam through his mind as he battled in this surprise attack.

Poppy didn't realize that she was down to one potion and had no food left in her inventory when she was struck by a blue soldier's sword. She had one heart left and no way to replenish her health. The only potion in her inventory was a potion of harming. She splashed it on one of the soldiers, which weakened him but didn't destroy him.

Anya spotted Poppy from across the room and

noticed she was down to one heart. She ordered her soldiers to end the attack.

"There is no more fighting. Please take the prisoners to their new home." She walked over to Poppy and said, "You are coming with me."

Poppy looked at her friends being led in another direction and asked, "What do you want from me?"

"You know what I want," Anya said. "I want you to build the skyscraper."

"I can't do it alone."

"I know," said Anya. "I found a team to work with you. They are handpicked from across the Overworld and from various time periods. Unlike you, they didn't put up a fight. They thought it was an honor to build a skyscraper for me."

Poppy didn't respond. She followed Anya to the castle and looked around for her friends. Anya noted, "If you're looking for your friends, they aren't here."

Anya led Poppy into a room where there were other people still dressed in their old skins. "This is your new team," said Anya.

Poppy didn't recognize any of these people. She wondered what time periods they came from. She also wondered how all of this was left out of history books. She had learned about the ice age, but it was just seen as a freak occurrence. There was no mention of Anya and her control over the ice age. Anya said, "You are all about to start on the skyscraper. I will lead you to the spot where I want it to be built, and I will provide you with all of the supplies."

A girl with red braids said to Poppy, "You're Poppy, right?"

"Yes," Poppy replied. "Why do you ask?"

"Anya has been waiting for you for a long time. We have been in this room for ages. She has been trying to track you down. I am so glad you are finally here so we can start and finish this project."

"What do you think will happen to us when the project is finished?" Poppy asked the girl.

"We'll probably build something else," she replied.

Another person added, "We will be her team of personal builders."

Anya overheard their conversation. "You are my team of builders. This is your job forever."

Poppy wasn't happy about being trapped with Anya, and she had to find a way out. She wondered where the people who had turned against Poppy had gone. She hoped they were planning an attack. However, she couldn't just wait around for someone else to save her. She had to think of her own plan. She didn't know what she was capable of doing since she only had one heart. Anya was also keeping a close eye on them, so she couldn't plan an uprising with the other builders.

"This is where I want the skyscraper to be built," Anya said as they approached a large patch of land near a frozen farm.

"I don't understand why you are freezing the Overworld," said Poppy as she stared at the farm. "It doesn't make any sense to me."

"Don't concern yourself with what I am doing.

Your only job is to build this skyscraper," said Anya as she handed Poppy supplies.

Poppy started to craft the foundation for the skyscraper. She hated to admit that she enjoyed building it. Despite being captured and in another time period, she was happy as she built the skyscraper. She stopped thinking of being cold and Anya watching her as she worked with the team to construct this mammoth skyscraper, which was to be much bigger than the one she had just built. She also knew this would be hard work, but it appeared as if she had a good team.

The girl with braids said, "Is she going to stick around and watch us build all day?"

"I guess so," Poppy said as she looked at Anya.

Anya walked over to them. "This isn't a social event. This is work, and I don't want you talking." Anya looked at the building's foundation and then looked at Poppy, who was running low on energy. Poppy didn't remember the last time she had eaten. Anya pulled out an apple and gave it to Poppy. Poppy took a bite, and her body felt reenergized. She didn't realize how hungry she had been. She missed picking apples off of trees and eating whenever she felt like it. Now that her hunger was satiated, she was able to build faster. She wanted to finish this skyscraper as quickly as she could, but she understood these things took time.

As Poppy placed the windows on the first floor of the skyscraper, she heard a voice call out in the distance.

"Help!" the voice screamed.

Poppy thought it sounded like Brett. She wanted

to run to him, but Anya was standing beside her and pointed her diamond sword into Poppy's back.

"You aren't going anywhere. You can't help anyone. You are just here to build," Anya said as she pressed the sword into Poppy's back.

"Help!" the voice called out again. This time it was much closer, and Poppy knew it was Brett.

"I have to help my friend," Poppy said.

"You don't have to do anything. You can only do what I tell you, and I am telling you that you must build this skyscraper." This time when Anya spoke she pierced Poppy's unarmored back, and Poppy felt a stinging pain radiate down her spine.

"Okay, I will just build," said Poppy as she placed a window and ignored her friend's call for help.

The cries grew more desperate, and Poppy couldn't stand by and do nothing. Poppy whispered to the girl with the braids, "Can you help me?"

"How?" asked he girl.

"I told you to stop talking!" Anya walked over and slammed her diamond sword into both of them.

Poppy was left with one heart, and she lacked the energy to help Brett. Tears filled her eyes. She had to help her friend, but wasn't sure how until she saw Cara quietly walk behind Anya. Cara swung her sword at Anya's back, and Anya wailed.

"It's over, Anya," said Cara. "We are destroying the command blocks right now."

"I don't believe you," Anya said as she turned around and tried to swing her sword at Cara, but Pete ran over and stopped Anya. He swung his sword at Anya's arm, and she cried.

"Believe us," Cara said.

Poppy heard Brett cry for help and raced toward the sound of his voice. She hoped she had enough energy to help him.

16
NEW CRIMINALS

Three people surrounded Brett, pointing their swords at him. Brett alternated between crying for help and trying to talk a group of three out of attacking him.

"I haven't done anything to you. I don't even know who you are," explained Brett.

One of the people surrounding him said, "We are treasure hunters, and we are going to take everything from this town. This means we are also going to empty your inventory."

"I have nothing left," he said.

"Show us," said a person in a red shirt and a hat.

Brett showed them what he had left in his inventory. It consisted of a few pieces of wheat, one glass of milk, a diamond sword, a bow and arrow, and an emerald. "Take whatever you want."

"This isn't much," they said as they looked through his inventory.

"Nobody has anything," Poppy said.

The group of three turned around, and one of them lunged toward Poppy and pressed his diamond sword against her back.

"I only have one heart left. If you strike me with this sword, I am gone. But before you destroy me, I have a plan that can help all of us," said Poppy bravely.

"Plan? Why should we work with you?" a nameless member of this new criminal team exclaimed.

"If you work with us to defeat Anya, she has a large collection of goods. We don't want those goods. We just want to defeat her," explained Poppy.

"Who is Anya? And why don't you want any of her treasures? It doesn't make any sense," said the criminal who still had his sword pressed against Poppy's back.

"Anya is in charge of this town, and she is also responsible for the ice age. She has trapped me here and is forcing me to build a skyscraper. I want to go home. I'm not here to collect souvenirs from this trip," replied Poppy.

The three treasure-hunting criminals looked at each other, and one replied, "Okay, we will help you defeat Anya."

Brett and Poppy led them to the castle. When they arrived, they saw their old friends battling Anya and her diminishing army of blue soldiers. As the gang battled the remaining soldiers, they started to feel warm.

Pete exclaimed, "They did it! They destroyed the command blocks!"

Anya let out a gasp. "How could they? I want it to be cold."

Poppy looked down at the grass. The icy film that covered the ground had faded, and the grass was wet and muddy. She didn't mind fighting in the mud because she was happy the ice age was officially over.

As their makeshift army captured Anya, Pete said in disbelief, "I am witnessing history. This is real, serious history. I am here as the ice age ends." He then added, "I must write an article, or maybe even a book, about this event. This is one of the biggest moments in the history of the Overworld."

Nobody was listening to Pete. Once Anya was defeated, Carl and Alexandra started to bicker. They were in the middle of a loud argument about finding a portal home.

"Now that Anya is defeated, it's time to leave," yelled Alexandra.

"I know, but we don't have to go home this second," said Carl. "We should try to help the people of the town."

"We've helped them enough," hollered Alexandra.

Everyone stood and watched the pair argue. Even Anya had her mouth open and was aghast at the situation.

Poppy said, "Why are you guys fighting? There is nothing to fight about. We have to celebrate."

"No we don't," said Anya. "You've destroyed my world."

"No," said Poppy, "we saved your world. In time you will see what you were doing to the Overworld was cruel and controlling. You were stopping crops from sprouting. You were destroying nature and creating the famine that was responsible for so many people starving."

Cara said, "You have no idea how hard it was to live in a constant state of hunger. You never felt that because you controlled all the food, but there were many times when I would dream about an apple and wake up and realize that I might never eat one again. You have no idea how that feels."

Anya didn't say anything for a while, and finally she uttered the words everyone had longed to hear, "I'm sorry."

Pete said, "I don't know how you got away with this in the past. There is no record of you in our time period, but I am going to change that. I want to write an article so people can learn that one person can impact the entire Overworld and that we must work together to make sure that people with this type of power don't abuse it."

"I'd like to read that article," said Alexandra.

"Me too," said Carl.

"Look, we agree on that," Alexandra told Carl.

As Poppy led Anya into the castle, she said, "I have one last building project, and then we can look for a portal."

"Are you building my skyscraper?" asked Anya.

"No," said Poppy. "I'm building a bedrock prison for you."

17
PASSAGE THROUGH TIME

Anya protested, but she knew it was pointless. Half of her army had turned against her, and the other half was defeated. She followed Poppy into the castle and awaited her imprisonment.

Poppy was surprised when she heard Anya say, "Can I offer you suggestions on how to build my prison? I always wanted to be a builder, but I was never any good at it. I'd love to work with you on this project."

"Of course," said Poppy.

Poppy and Anya walked past Anya's throne and to the changing room. Poppy said, "This is where we are going to build the prison. It will remind you that you should never force people to change skins for you."

Anya didn't say anything. She just watched Poppy construct a bedrock wall. Poppy stopped. "I thought you wanted to work on this with me? I can teach you how to build."

Anya said, “Thank you. I’d love it if we could build a window. I would hate not to be able to see the sun rise and set.”

“Now that your command blocks are broken, you can see everything in bloom. Before you had created a world where nothing could grow.”

“I know I was a bad person,” Anya said as she watched Poppy build a wall with a window.

Brett, Joe, Pete, Carl, and Alexandra sprinted into the castle. Brett asked, “How long do you think this will take?”

Poppy looked at the wall. She still had to create a door and another wall. “Not much longer.”

Cara and Claudia walked into the room. Poppy asked them, “Would you like to help me finish building this?”

They replied, “Yes,” in unison.

Poppy said, “After it’s done, we are going to need someone to help watch Anya and make sure she gets meals. Would you be able to help with that?”

“Yes,” said Cara. “I am so glad to be home and to be able to grow wheat and be with my friends. I will do anything in order to have peace in the Overworld and live the life I always loved.”

“Me too. I will help out,” said Claudia.

As Poppy finished the bedrock prison, she could hear Alexandra and Carl bickering.

“We have to find the portal now. I want to go home,” said Alexandra.

“We will find the portal. You just have to be patient,” said Carl.

"I don't want to be patient. I want to be searching for the portal," Alexandra said, raising her voice.

Nobody told them to stop fighting. Everyone was used to it, but they had to learn how to communicate properly. The gang was surprised when Anya, who was in the middle of an interview with Pete, said, "Alexandra and Carl, those are your names, right?"

"Yes," they replied.

"You can't fight all the time. It's rather exhausting for us to hear, and you guys probably don't like it too much either."

Alexandra and Carl looked at each other. Their faces were red. They were embarrassed. They apologized for their behavior and continued to talk to each other in a normal respectful tone.

Pete restarted his interview. "What made you build the command blocks? Why did you choose to dress in blue and have all of your soldiers dress the same?"

"I love the cold weather," confessed Anya, "and I wanted it to be cold every day. I didn't care what happened to the crops because I was able to build an indoor farm. I thought everyone would be able to do the same."

"Just because you like something doesn't mean everyone likes it," said Pete.

"I know," said Anya. "I'm beginning to realize that now."

Poppy announced, "It's done. It's time to go into the prison."

Pete said, "Just one more question."

Anya asked, "What is it?"

"Do you regret everything you've done?"

Anya walked into the bedrock prison. "Yes," she said solemnly, and Poppy closed the door to the prison.

They said goodbye to Claudia and Cara and walked out of the castle in search of the portal.

"Do you think it will be easy to find?" asked Pete.

"We've been back in time before, and it's not easy to get home, but we always get there," said Poppy. Poppy's heart beat rapidly when she thought about going home. She hoped the skyscraper wasn't destroyed. She wanted to celebrate its grand opening. She laughed at how nervous she used to be to speak in front of the crowd about the construction. Now she looked forward to talking to people, to feasting, and to plotting with Brett for new pranks she could pull on her old friends. She wanted to be back in Meadow Mews.

Alexandra stumbled upon an opening to a mine. "Do you think there might be a portal in here? You know there are usually holes in mines, and maybe we can dig something deeper that could create one."

"That's a good idea," said Brett.

Joe added, "We have found portals in mines before, and they worked quite well."

Pete was writing notes for his article on time travel. He walked behind the gang as they searched for portals in the mine.

"I think I found something," said Joe as he banged his pickaxe against the ground and a burst of cold air rushed toward him.

"Are you sure?" Alexandra was excited.

"I hope so," said Joe as he hopped in the hole and hoped he'd land in Meadow Mews in the right time period.

Brett jumped in after him. The frigid air created instant goose bumps on Brett's arms as he traveled through this portal. The farther he fell, the more he hoped he would land in the middle of Meadow Mews. He was suspicious because he felt they came across the portal too easily, but he reminded himself that they had become skilled at time travel and they knew how to detect portals a lot faster than they did in the past. Another blast of icy-cold air burst though the portal. Normally the cold would bother him, but today he found it comforting. He had a smile on his face. He was going home.

18

GRAND REOPENING

The portal seemed to take longer than usual, and Brett was getting impatient. He called out to his friends to see if they were still close by, but there was no response. He wanted to land, and when he finally did, he wasn't sure where he had landed.

Brett fell to the ground with a thump and explored the area. He arrived in a swampy biome and in the middle of the day. It was hot, which made Brett happy. He'd had enough of the cold and was glad to be warm. He took out a map and spotted Meadow Mews across the Overworld. He scanned for Poppy and found that she was in Meadow Mews and teleported to her.

Poppy was standing in front of the skyscraper assessing the damage. "This can be repaired," she said to Helen and Nancy, "but it's going to take a few days."

"We will plan for a grand opening celebration in a week. Does that work?" asked Helen.

"Yes," Poppy replied when she saw Brett walk toward her.

"Do you need any help?" he asked.

"I'd love some," said Poppy.

Joe, Pete, Alexandra, and Carl hurried over to them. "We're back!" they announced.

Alexandra said, "We have to go back to our town. We only came here for the grand opening celebration, and now that it's over, we must go home."

Poppy said, "It's not over, it hasn't even begun. I have to rebuild, and then we will have the celebration in a week."

Carl suggested to Alexandra, "Perhaps we should stick around for the celebration."

"We don't have a place to stay," Alexandra reminded him.

Brett said, "If you guys don't bicker, you can stay at my house."

"That is so nice of you," said Carl.

"We promise, we won't fight," said Alexandra.

Brett hoped they could keep that promise. He announced, "I am going to help Poppy rebuild the skyscraper."

"Can we help?" asked Carl.

"The more people who can help me, the quicker we can finish," said Poppy.

Joe asked, "Has there been any damage to the rooftop farm?"

"Let's see," said Poppy.

The gang entered the skyscraper. The first floor

had windows missing, and the floor was charred. They climbed the stairs, stopping at each floor to inspect the damage. The higher floors had no damage at all, but everyone was nervous when they reached the roof. They weren't sure if Anya's soldiers had destroyed the roof while they were in the past.

Brett closed his eyes. He didn't want to know what the rooftop farm looked like; he was too nervous. He finally opened them when he heard Joe say, "Wow, I forgot how nice it is to just grab a fresh apple from a tree and take a bite."

Poppy picked an apple from a tree and stood underneath the hot sun. "I had also forgotten how nice it is to feel the heat on my skin."

Pete stood next to them and took notes. He wasn't picking apples off the trees, but was watching the gang as they ate their fruit. He remarked, "We take a lot of things for granted. I am so glad to be back. I'm also glad that people will get to read about this part of history. It's important that Anya not be forgotten." Pete then said, "I am going to have to say goodbye."

"Aren't you writing an article about the grand opening celebration for the skyscraper?" asked Poppy.

"I will be back in a week, but now I have to go find the town where Anya lived. I want to find her in the bedrock prison and interview her. I want to see how she feels."

"I can't wait to read that article," said Brett.

Pete left, and the gang got to work. The group spent their days repairing all the damage. After a week of hard work, the skyscraper was repaired and ready to open. Helen and Nancy had planned a large grand opening ceremony. The day arrived for the celebration, and Poppy stared at the crowd there to hear her address them. She looked at the podium and realized that her heart wasn't beating as fast as it normally did in those situations. She wasn't nervous at all. She was confident and excited to tell people about the construction of this mammoth building.

As Poppy stood on the podium and addressed the crowd, she spotted Pete standing alongside a familiar face in the crowd. He had found Anya, interviewed her, and brought her back through a portal with him. When Poppy's speech was over, Pete and Anya approached Poppy.

Anya said, "I just wanted you to know that I apologize for everything I did. I spent some time in that bedrock prison thinking about what I've done wrong. While I was in prison, Cara brought me food every day. One morning she asked if I wanted to help her build, and we started working together. Soon I became a skilled builder. Now I know how hard it is to construct things, and I'm sorry for destroying parts of the skyscraper. You did a good job rebuilding."

Poppy said, "Thank you," and invited Anya to the celebration. That afternoon everyone ate, danced, and celebrated until dark.

The End